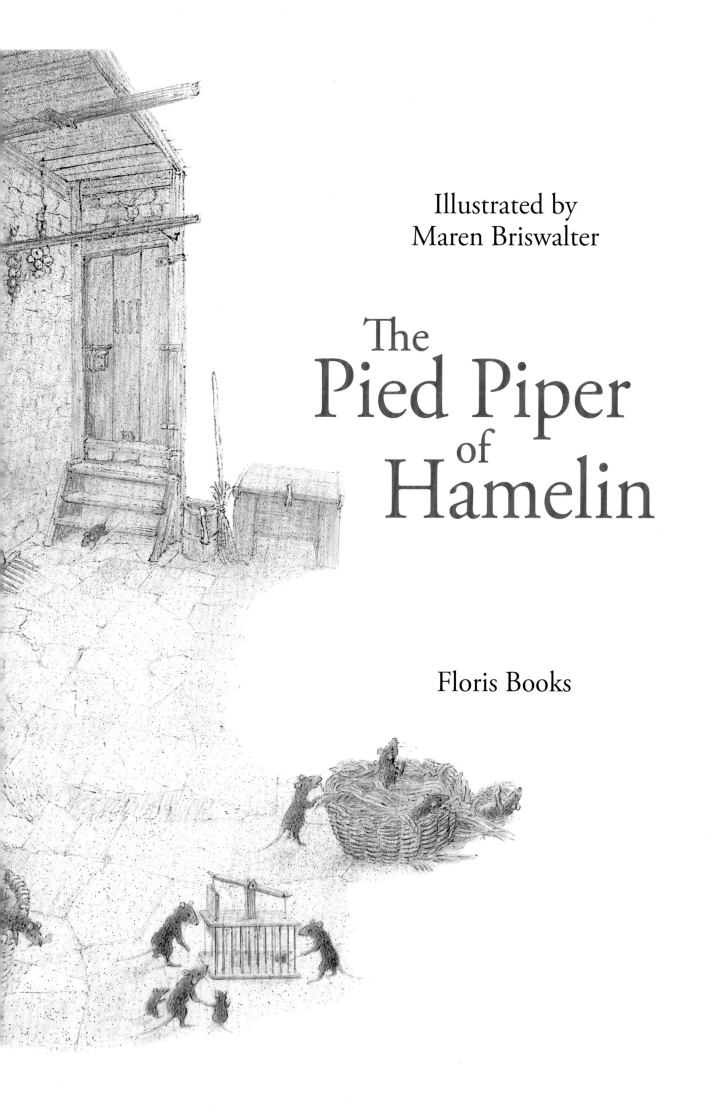

Illustrated by
Maren Briswalter

The
Pied Piper
of
Hamelin

Floris Books

In Germany, beside a great river, is a town called Hamelin. Hundreds of years ago, Hamelin was rich and happy. But then, early one summer, it was overrun by a plague of rats.

There were rats everywhere, in every house and building. They were in the parlours and cellars, bedrooms and kitchens, cupboards and attics. There were not enough cats or traps to catch them, and their numbers kept growing.

They ate all the food, then started on the cloth, and even gnawed the wood.

The people were worrying about what to do,
when a stranger arrived. He was wearing
clothes made of brightly coloured patches.

He went to the town hall and said, "If I get
rid of all the rats in Hamelin, will you pay me a
thousand silver coins?"

"Yes, yes, we certainly will!" the people replied.

So the stranger took a flute from his pocket and began to play a beautiful, haunting tune. As he played, the rats came to him: hundreds and hundreds of them, spilling from buildings, scampering out of drains and filling the street.

Still playing the beautiful, haunting tune,
the Pied Piper walked out of the town,
beyond the city walls and into the great
river.

Every single rat followed, swarming after
him into the water, where they were swept
away and drowned. There was not
one rat left in the whole of Hamelin.

The people celebrated, delighted to be free of the rats.
But they soon went back to their normal lives.
They had seen how quickly and easily the Pied Piper
had led the rats out and they did not want to
give him the thousand silver coins. They thought of
all sorts of excuses and, in the end, refused to
pay him at all.

"You will regret this!" he told them angrily.
And then he left.

Just after midsummer, the Pied Piper returned, wearing a red hunting hat. He took out his flute and began to play another beautiful, mysterious tune.

This time, as he played, the children came to him: all the girls and boys of Hamelin, tumbling out of houses, skipping through the streets and filling the air with laughter.

Young children and older children – they all danced along behind the Pied Piper.

Still playing the beautiful, mysterious tune, the Pied Piper walked out of the town, beside the river, over the fields and meadows and into the hills. Every single child followed him.

A nursemaid carrying a little child was tired and fell behind. She watched the children follow the Pied Piper through an opening in the side of a hill, then she turned back.

One boy was cold and went home to get his coat, but then the opening in the hill had closed. He missed the Piper's music his whole life.

All the other children of Hamelin were gone.

The people of the town searched everywhere for their children, crying and shouting. They sent messengers out on horse and by ship, looking for their daughters and sons.

But they never found them.

One hundred and thirty children disappeared that day.

Many years passed before the merry voices of other children were heard in Hamelin. Even now, years and years later, no music is allowed on the street the children followed out of town. If a bride is walking to her wedding, the musicians must stop playing on that street.

A thousand silver coins would have been nothing compared to the terrible price the people of Hamelin paid to the Pied Piper.